STOP THIEF!

Quick, Joe. Shove in the fake pearl and let's get out of here . . .

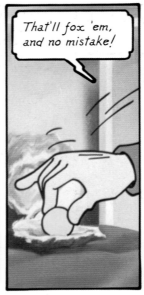

That'll fox 'em, and no mistake!

Back to the car now . . . don't hang around!

A close shave. Seconds later the guards rush back, with the Director of the Museum . . .

Oh sir, sir! It's terrible! A disaster!

What sort of tomfoolery is this? There's the pearl, perfectly safe . . .

What the . . . ? I could have sworn . . .

No, wait! . . . This has happened elsewhere. I've heard about it from colleagues in other museums . . .

I know I'm right, sir . . . The pearl went . . . and came back!

These are the only witnesses! If only they could talk . . .

Based on the characters created by Hergé

EGMONT

The TINTIN books are published in the following languages:

Alsacien	CASTERMAN
Basque	ELKAR
Bengali	ANANDA
Bernese	EMMENTALER DRUCK
Breton	AN HERE
Catalan	CASTERMAN
Chinese	CASTERMAN/CHINA CHILDREN PUBLISHING
Corsican	CASTERMAN
Danish	CARLSEN
Dutch	CASTERMAN
English	EGMONT UK LTD/LITTLE, BROWN & CO.
Esperanto	ESPERANTIX/CASTERMAN
Finnish	OTAVA
French	CASTERMAN
Gallo	RUE DES SCRIBES
Gaumais	CASTERMAN
German	CARLSEN
Greek	CASTERMAN
Hebrew	MIZRAHI
Indonesian	INDIRA
Italian	CASTERMAN
Japanese	FUKUINKAN
Korean	CASTERMAN/SOL
Latin	ELI/CASTERMAN
Luxembourgeois	IMPRIMERIE SAINT-PAUL
Norwegian	EGMONT
Picard	CASTERMAN
Polish	CASTERMAN/MOTOPOL
Portuguese	CASTERMAN
Provençal	CASTERMAN
Romanche	LIGIA ROMONTSCHA
Russian	CASTERMAN
Serbo-Croatian	DECJE NOVINE
Spanish	CASTERMAN
Swedish	CARLSEN
Thai	CASTERMAN
Tibetan	CASTERMAN
Turkish	YAPI KREDI YAYINLARI

TRANSLATED BY
LESLIE LONSDALE-COOPER AND MICHAEL TURNER

EGMONT
We bring stories to life

Artwork copyright © 1973 by Editions Casterman, Paris and Tournai.
Copyright © renewed 1973 by Casterman.
Text copyright © 1973 by Egmont UK Limited.
First published in Great Britain in 1973 by Methuen Children's Books.
This edition published in 2014 by Egmont UK Limited,
The Yellow Building, 1 Nicholas Road, London W11 4AN
www.egmont.co.uk
Stay safe online. Egmont is not responsible
for content hosted by third parties.

Hardback: ISBN 978 1 4052 0822 2
Paperback: ISBN 978 1 4052 0634 1

Next day, at Klow airport in Syldavia, a B714 comes in to land . . .

Among the passengers are Tintin, Snowy and Captain Haddock.

Here we are, Captain. Out we get!

But the Customs are waiting. The Captain's golf bag gets a thorough search.

Golf! . . . Nothing to declare! . . . You compris? . . . Golf club . . . hit, hit . . . little ball . . . Understand?

Naturally, sir. You may proceed. Welcome to Syldavia.

Blistering barnacles! Idiots! Just a few harmless golf clubs!

Oh! So sorry!

Great snakes! Thomson and Thompson! What on earth are they doing in Syldavia?

Are you here on holiday too? We're off to see Professor Calculus, on Lake Pollishoff!

Holiday? No! Quite the opposite! A secret mission!

To be precise: dumb's the word for us!

Transit passengers Tintin, Snowy and Captain Haddock please report to desk number twenty for details of their air taxi reservations.

Good. Can we give you a lift anywhere?

Your pilot is waiting for you now, Mr Tintin.

Thank you.

Thundering typhoons!

Are you coming, Captain?

Just a minute . . .

Soon the travellers are high above the fierce Syldavian mountains . . .

You have a friend living by Lake Pollishoff? How strange . . .

There it is . . . an artificial lake. They submerged a whole village to make it . . . There's a curse on it, Mr Tintin. Nothing but bad luck . . . an evil place!

What's the matter? . . . Something's wrong!

FTTT

FTTT

The starboard engine begins to splutter . . . coughs . . . and finally . . . dies.

We're done for! . . . Engine's kaput! . . . Jump!

The passengers watch dumbfounded as the pilot, his parachute ready, leaps from the plane.

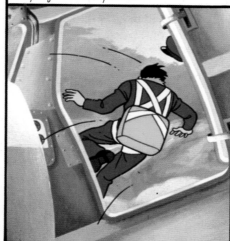

Tintin keeps his head. In a flash he is in the pilot's seat . . .

Jump? Us? Without parachutes? . . . You're crazy! . . . Hi! You! . . . Come back here!

Tintin fights desperately to regain control . . . and dodges between huge mountain peaks . . . Lower and lower, past towering crags . . .

I'm going to try to land her in that valley . . . Under-carriage down . . . Hang on, here we go!

Wheels slam into the rocky ground, tyres scream and burst. One wing torn away, the plane hurtles on to destruction . . .

Skidding wildly towards a precipice . . . it stops, poised over the abyss . . .

WOOAH! WOOAH!

Help! The plane's rocking . . . We're going over!!

No! Two well-aimed ropes are suddenly flung over the battered tail . . .

In the nick of time! Two children, passing in a donkey-cart, have spotted the damaged aircraft and come to the rescue.

Pull, Gustav, pull!!

St. Vladimir! The engines are on fire! Quick, run for it!

Tintin, Snowy and Captain Haddock are safely out . . . Now only the Thompsons are left on board . . .

After you, my dear Thomson . . .

To be precise: you first, my dear Thompson . . .

Suddenly . . .

The plane plunges forward . . . As it goes, the detectives are flung through the door . . .

OOOPS!

The aircraft smashes into the ravine and explodes . . . Debris scatters in all directions.

Lucky for us you were here! My name is Tintin. These are my friends: Captain Haddock, Mr Thompson and Mr Thomson. And this is Snowy.

I am called Niko, and this is my sister, Nushka.

We were on our way to visit a friend . . . Cuthbert Calculus . . . He lives in the Villa Sprog, by the lake.

The Villa Sprog! . . . You mustn't go! . . . The lake is a bad place!

Despite the warning the travellers climb into the cart and set off with the children towards the Villa Sprog ... But, high on a cliff, someone is watching them ... Their pilot!

Vulture Four calling Neptune ... Operation Sardine unsuccessful. Customers heading for rendezvous two ... Over and out!

Winding their way through the hills the travellers come at last to the Villa Sprog, built on the lakeside.

Here you are at last! I was getting quite worried!

Dear old Cuthbert! Blistering barnacles, it's good to see you!

Thank you again for everything ... We'll see you tomorrow?

The Captain doesn't waste time: he heads for the bar ...

I'm dry as a bone after all that cliff hanging! I need a whisky ...

YOW!

Billions of bilious blue blistering barnacles ... What's this? ... An indoor mirage?!

The bar was just a three-dimensional image. I'm trying out this machine ... I'll explain everything while we have supper. Madame Flik, my housekeeper, has prepared a special savoury szlaszek ... So come and sit down.

Now, Professor, tell us about your phantom furniture.

Certainly not ... just simple diapositives. What I'm trying to create are sort of photocopies in relief.

But it's absolutely top secret ... there are greedy people about ...

Aha! Forgers!

What?!

What forgers?

More and more works of art are being stolen, all over the world . . . Thieves take an original, and leave behind a forgery . . .

At first, they used nothing but crude copies . . .

But in recent months it's taken an expert to spot the fakes, they're so good!

Anyway, Professor, let's enjoy our holiday with you, in spite of the journey!

You must be very tired. Madame Flik will show you your rooms.

Captain Haddock and the Thompsons are soon asleep, but Tintin lies awake puzzling over the day's events.

Oh well, it's no good worrying ourselves . . . Good night, Snowy, sleep well.

All is quiet . . .

. . . when . . . suddenly . . .

KRIIK-KRIIK

KRIIK-KRIIK

Hello! . . . What's that noise? . . . Some sort of night owl, I suppose . . .

But the sound is coming from the well-head, where someone is turning the handles . . . Madame Flik!

KRIIK-KRIIK

KRIIK-KRIIK

The bucket brings up a strange load . . . a walkie-talkie!

Agent Rameses calling King Shark! . . . Calling King Shark! . . .

Agent Rameses reporting ... Customers have arrived after all ...

King Shark receiving you, Rameses. Vulture reported arrival. Operation Crab will commence tomorrow. Proceed as arranged ... Over and out!

Madame Flik signs off. She has her orders!

Next morning Niko and Nushka come to the Villa, to take Tintin exploring.

Hello! Good morning!

Ready to go, Tintin?

It's very peaceful here.

Oh, yes. No one ever comes this way.

Laughing and talking, Tintin and the children make their way along a path leading to the cliff top. Snowy and Gustav prefer to go down to the lake.

Meanwhile, at the Villa Sprog, Captain Haddock visits the professor in his laboratory.

Very odd ... I could have sworn I left my notes on that table last night ... You haven't seen them, have you, Captain?

Me? Your notes? No ...

But in another room, downstairs ...

Ha! ha! our clever professor shouldn't leave things lying about! I'll hide the bottle here, with his papers inside ... Crab will soon take care of them ...

Scarcely has Madame Flik turned her back, before the bottle, papers and all, vanishes into thin air!

But it soon reappears ... in the hands of a frogman climbing out of the well ...

There we are! Job done, no problems!

But suddenly ...

WOOAH! WOOAH!

Filthy luck! I've been spotted!

Thundering typhoons! What's going on down there? ...

Blue blistering barnacles! ...It's Snowy, fighting with a frogman! ...

GRRR!

Hang on, Snowy! I'm coming! Look out, Captain!

OOPS!

Thundering typhoons! What was the pirate up to?

A pirate? ...I thought he was a frogman.

He's dropped a kipper ...er, flopped a slipper ...no, slopped a...

...a flipper!

In the meantime, Tintin, Niko and Nushka wander along the cliff...

Whatever makes you say the lake is evil? It's beautiful!

Don't be too sure, Tintin! It's beautiful, and dangerous!

RRRRR

Hello! ...What can that be?

KLOWKA-KOLA

Why an advertising plane in this outlandish spot?

Target in view! ...OK... Shooting now!

Meanwhile, not very far away...

Ah! Excellent camera-work! ...So there you are, my dear Tintin! ...If only you knew what lies in store for you! ...Ha! ha! ha! ha!

Beside the mysterious observer two frogmen wait . . .

You saw them? . . . The one with the tuft of hair is Tintin . . . He is extremely dangerous! . . . Operation Crab goes ahead. You have your orders. Use the new laughing gas!

Tintin returns to the Villa Sprog. Immediately Captain Haddock tells him of the morning's events. Tintin listens carefully.

Part of a flipper torn off by Snowy . . . The professor's lost papers . . . It all begins to make sense . . .

Now we've got this bit of rubber, perhaps the dogs can track the frogman's route . . .

Tintin follows Snowy, leaving the Thompsons to guard the villa. The Captain goes after Gustav, who also seems to have picked up a trail . . . Snowy makes the first discovery: a metal ring half buried in the ground. Tense with excitement, Tintin pulls. Slowly, quietly, a section of rock slides open, to reveal the entrance to a cave . . .

Great snakes! A secret passage . . . with a staircase . . . All right, let's go!

Down the first few steps, then suddenly . . .

Oh!! The door's shut! . . . I can't get out! . . . But Snowy managed to escape . . . I'll have to go on . . . nothing else I can do . . .

THUD

At the foot of the staircase, an amazing sight greets Tintin . . .

What in the world?! Treasures!! Can they be . . . stolen from museums, like the Thompsons said?

That's up to the Syldavian police . . . I must find a way out . . .

Light! . . . I'm sure this cave must be connected to the lake . . .

Taking a deep breath, Tintin dives . . .

!!Help! . . . A wire grille! . . . I'm trapped!!

Tintin wrestles desperately with the metal strands, the air draining slowly from his lungs. Just in time Snowy sees bubbles on the lake surface and dives to the rescue.

At last the wires give way!

Good old Snowy! That was a near thing!

Meanwhile, at the villa...

Professor, what does your funny machine make?

Cream cake? No, it's a special paste, which I put here with the detectives' hats there on the other side.

I switch on the current, and ... hey presto!

There! Duplicate hats! Absolutely indistinguishable... You may try them on, gentlemen.

But... I... It's all sticky!...

To be precise: we're all stuck up!

Yes, I'm afraid you are. I haven't yet discovered how to stabilize the reproductions, but...

... it's only a matter of days...

BANG

The laughing gas is working!... Quick, grab the children and get out... Hurry!

HA! HA!

HA! HA!

HA! HA!

Tintin and Snowy are on the way home...

Look! Someone's attacking the house!

They're kidnapping Niko and Nushka! . . . Quick, Snowy!

HA! HA!

HI! HI! HI!

Ah, there you are, Captain. I'm afraid we're too late.

Yes, by thunder! Their launch is already well offshore.

Greetings, my dear Tintin. Your young friends will come to no harm, provided of course you obey my orders precisely!

It's a taped message from the kidnappers!

I know the Professor's machine is nearly completed. I want that machine, Tintin . . . and you are going to hand it over to me!

HA! HA! . . . OH! HO! HO!

In two days' time, at midday, on the southern shore . . . You will come alone, and unarmed. And you won't go to the police!

Pirate!

I've heard that voice before, somewhere . . .

AH! HA! HA!

We have a powerful adversary . . . and I'm sure we're being watched! We must comb the house from top to bottom. There's bound to be a secret passage somewhere.

A frantic search begins . . . all join in the hunt . . .

WOOAH! WOOAH!

The clock, Snowy? You think so?

Let's try this knob . . . OH!!

Here, Captain! . . . This is certainly how the kidnappers got in!

!

You stay, Captain, while I take a look . . .

All right. But mind how you go!

Meanwhile, from high on the mountainside two spies have the Villa Sprog under observation . . .

It's almost reporting time for Rameses.

Our visitors are getting too inquisitive. I must warn King Shark.

Meanwhile . . .

. . . A door? . . . Where does it lead?

Great snakes! The bottom of the well! . . . With a transmitter sitting in the water-bucket!

Now what's old Mother Flik up to, I wonder?

HOOO!

Spies have changed quite a bit since the days of Mata Hari, eh Madame Flik? . . . Come on! Back to the villa!

Can't raise a cheep out of Rameses . . . I wonder what's going on? . . .

Madame Flik? A spy? . . . I can't believe it's true.

Now then, who do you work for? . . . Spill the beans, you snooping old sea-trout, or you'll . . .

It's no good, Captain. Madame Flik certainly won't know her boss's real name. There's only one thing to do . . .

We must call in the police . . . But how can we leave the villa without being seen? . . . Let me think . . . Aha!

And while Tintin outlines his plan, Niko and Nushka are taken by their captors before King Shark.

Don't you dare lay a finger on my sister!

Big words! . . . A proper little Tintin! . . . All right . . . out! Throw them in the cooler!

The frogmen drag the children to a damp cellar and lock them in. No escape!

Boohoo! . . . No one . . . sniff . . . will ever find us . . . sniff . . . in this awful place! . . .

Ssh, Nushka. Don't cry. Trust Tintin. He'll save us, you'll see.

Sitting in the control room, King Shark issues his orders . . .

This is King Shark. Keep your eyes skinned!

Sever their communications!

We'd better get busy: we must cut the telephone wires.

Meanwhile . . .

Take care of yourself, Tintin.

Provided the Thompsons keep rolling, it'll go like clockwork!

On the hill, the observers maintain their watch . . .

Tell the boss they're still there, marching up and down like toy soldiers.

Phew! . . . So, this is what he meant by "Get down to it!"

To be precise, he certainly meant to get us down!

I must get word to the police somehow!

Ah! A farm. Let's hope there's someone at home!

Hello! Hello! Please open the door! I need to use the telephone!

Be off with you! If you don't go away...

THUMP THUMP

...I'll blow you to bits!

Not the friendliest farmer I've known...

BANG

That tramp is still outside, Ladislasz...

Yes... I shall telephone the politzskaia.

Hello?... Hello, politzski?... Hello?... Hello?...

But not far away...

Hello?... Hello?... By Ottokar! The telephone is dead!

They've cut the wires, that's for sure... Come on, Snowy, we must move!

Before long, Tintin and Snowy reach the main road to Klow.

A car's coming... Snowy, we're saved!

Hi! Stop!... Good heavens!... It can't be true!

16

Signora Bianca Castafiore!!

My dear young friend! What are you doing, all by yourself in the middle of nowhere?

I need your help, Signora. I must get to the nearest police station.

Then jump in! ... Avanti!

Speeding along with the opera star. Tintin soon reaches the town. Ever cautious, he suggests parking in a side street near the police station.

I just want to make sure the coast's clear ...

As I thought ... Two men watching the entrance ... I'll never get past them.

What can we do? I simply must get in!

Wait, I have an idea ... My accompanist, Mr Wagner, will help you out ...

A few minutes later ...

That's him! ... Look at the shape ... And the dog! ... Come on, Dumkluk, let's tail him!

Such silly men! Completely fooled by my little Mr Wagner in disguise! ... Now, off you go, caro mio.

Tintin is soon telling his story to the police chief, who listens carefully ...

Everything centres on the lake ... All your discoveries point to it ...

But half the water lies within the frontiers of Borduria ... So unfortunately ...

I see: possible diplomatic complications ... Look, give me a free hand, and a little practical support ... This is what I plan to do ...

Lake Pollishoff

My friend Professor Calculus once made a pocket-submarine: we used it to hunt for sunken treasure . . .

Two days later, at King Shark's headquarters . . .

A truck heading for the villa, boss . . . Do we stop it?

No, no, let it go. It'll be equipment for Calculus . . . and for us! Ha! ha! ha!

Inside the villa, the Captain is worried . . .

Blistering barnacles, where can he be?

No news is good news!

To be precise: no news is no good!

Captain! . . . Come quickly!

That's Calculus! . . . What!? . . .

This truck . . . it just appeared . . .

. . . with me inside! Hello!

Tintin! Am I glad to see you!

Look! . . . My submarine!

Tintin explains his plan to save Niko and Nushka . . . He'll keep the rendezvous with the kidnappers, while the Captain follows secretly underwater.

At last, preparations are complete . . .

Is it all ready, Professor?

No, it's all ready. It's a scale model of my machine.

Taking the box, Tintin sets off for the prearranged meeting place.

They'll be here soon . . . Which way will they come?

He's there . . . alone!

Calling King Shark! Calling King Shark! Tintin is at the rendezvous. Taking him aboard immediately... Over and out!

A submarine! Just as I thought!

As soon as Tintin has embarked, the submarine disappears beneath the waters of the lake.

Meanwhile, in a nearby cove...

All right...You understand? I'll be back as soon as I've found their hideout. Wait for me here!

Full ahead!

The Captain's manner can sometimes be a trifle...er...

...Dry?

The Captain follows the mysterious submarine, taking care not to be observed. But he loses his quarry among the ruins of the drowned village.

Blistering barnacles! Where's that bashi-bazouk gone to? There are dozens of hiding places down here!

But the submarine has already reached its destination.

Quite a set-up! You gangsters are obviously on to a good racket...For the moment!

Tintin is escorted to the control room...A shock awaits him. From the depths of an armchair comes an unexpected greeting.

So, my dear Tintin! We meet again!

?!!YOU!

The porthole's given way! Close the watertight doors! Hurry!

With a frightening crack the glass dissolves in smithereens. The lake floods in. More by luck than judgement, Niko pilots the tank out of its dock.

Yes, boss . . . With the tank . . . through the port-hole . . . Yes, boss . . . your unbreakable glass . . . Yes, boss . . . they broke it!

You blundering fools! I'll handle this myself! . . . Little ruffians!

Rastapopoulos monitors the movements of the underwater tank from the control room . . .

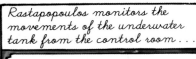

Look, Nushka, we're in the old village under the lake!

What's happening? The tank won't steer anymore . . . It's turning round . . . as if someone's taken control . . .

I'm frightened, Niko!

Ha! ha! ha! Rastapopoulos always has the last word, my little kiddywinks! . . . Home you come!

Diavolo! Where did that come from?

Captain Haddock, cruising down a street, almost collides with the tank . . .

Road-hogs! . . . It's my right of way!

It's Captain Haddock! . . . Captain, Captain, it's us!

Aaaghrr! A couple of salvoes will settle his hash! . . . Four, three, two . . .

Stop! You can't do that!

Hi! hi! hi! I'm going to enjoy this ... too good a chance to miss! ... Curtains for our bold sea-dog!

Merciless swine!

Grabbing the submarine captain, Tintin hurls him over his shoulder ...

The gangster lands with a crash on the control panel ...

Dozens of light signals whirl on dials ... With a single flash the pictures vanish from the television screens.

All King Shark's mechanical marvels suddenly go mad ... Chaos reigns ...

A second gangster aims his gun at Tintin ...

HUP!

YEOW!

The weapon sails away ... and lands on the controls ...

... automatically the tank fires a salvo of torpedoes ...

Oh, no! It's us! We're shooting at the Captain!

Thundering typhoons! I'm being attacked!

23

Help! The submarine's been hit... and I can't stop us firing these beastly torpedoes!

Disabled, the submarine settles helplessly on the bed of the lake.

Hooray! That's taken care of Bluebeard! ...Now it's your turn, my clever little tadpoles!

There you are! ... Good! Come along now ... He! he! Our little game is over!

While we wait for our bold buccaneer and his sister, I want to show you my little collection. Come, my dear Tintin!

Closely guarded by the Rasta-popoulos thugs, Tintin is taken to a vast gallery.

What do you think of them? ...Every one an original, all authentic, simply waiting for Professor Calculus's machine...

...to make thousands more authentic originals! Ha! ha! ha!

Your greed will finish you, Rastapopoulos!

And your tongue will be the end of you! Out!

At that moment, the underwater tank returns to its hangar.

We've failed!

Oh, poor Captain Haddock! . . . Whatever will Tintin say? . . .

Meanwhile . . .

Boss, the children have been recaptured.

Not now . . . I want to try out this lovely, lovely machine!

Let's start with something simple: a box of cigars, for example. I put it here . . . On the other side, some of the special paste . . .

Rastapopoulos presses a button . . . and the rays begin to do their work.

Ha! ha! Success! A perfect reproduction!

Er . . . the copy seems a bit big, to me . . .

Not at all! Look!

But . . . BUT . . . EEEEEEEEK!

GNAAAA

Listen to that! The boss doesn't sound in a very good temper!

Suddenly...

BOANG

What . . . what's happening? . . . Boss! . . . Boss! . . . Speak to me!

SABOTAGE! . . . I'VE BEEN DONE!

. . . BUT RASTAPOPOULOS GETS EVEN WITH PEOPLE WHO FOOL WITH HIM!

GLOP

Maddened with rage, Rastapopoulos hurls the children into a dark cellar . . .

Niko! Nushka! . . . That miserable gangster . . . He managed to recapture the tank . . .

Tintin!

Oh yes, there's your precious Tintin . . . and there he stays!

Boss! Boss! . . . Police! It's the police!

You call yourself King Shark. Rastapopoulos! Lord of the rats, more likely! You promised to free the children!

Yes, but in exchange for the genuine invention!

You thought you could fool me, eh? ... How wrong you were! ... Goodbye! ... And don't forget: in an hour's time ... BOOM!

My poor young friends: I think we're done for. We can't reach the switch, or immobilise the ball-cock ...

Meanwhile ...
You understand? Swimming in pairs, take the treasures back to the cave.

OK, boss!

Rastapopoulos's orders are swiftly carried out. The frogmen go to work, leaving the secret lair with their precious cargo.

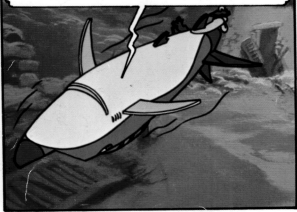

Not far away ...

Ten thousand thundering typhoons! The confounded engine won't go! ...What's to become of us now, Snowy, old fellow?! ...

I'll have one more try . . .

The Captain pushes the starter desperately. The propeller, jammed by the damaged rudder shakes violently but refuses to budge.

Suddenly, the twisted metal breaks loose and the propeller whirls into action.

Hooray! Up she rises! . . . We're sailing upsidedown, but never mind!

??Blistering barnacles! What are those seagherkins doing? . . . Out of my way, you duck-billed platypuses, you!

OOOPS!

Meanwhile . . .

Not a sign . . . He's drunk without a face . . . er . . . funked without a race . . . er . . . bunked to outer space . . .

Can you see the Captain?

Wait! I can see a shadow . . . coming up!

Take care! It might be the Loch Ness monster!

EEEEEEEK!

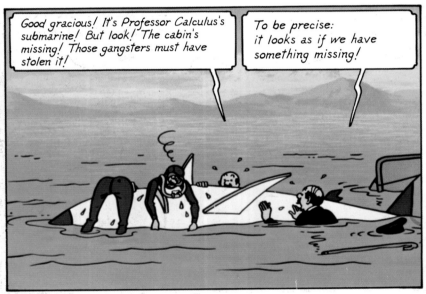

Good gracious! It's Professor Calculus's submarine! But look! The cabin's missing! Those gangsters must have stolen it!

To be precise: it looks as if we have something missing!

Captain! Where have you been?!

In Davey Jones's locker, blistering barnacles! Phew! Fresh air! I thought we'd never get out of that lobster-pot!

Look! We're saved! There's a launch coming to the rescue!

Syldavian River Police! . . . Which of you is Captain Haddock?

Me! . . . And I know where Tintin is!

Tintin, Niko and Nushka are being held prisoner by a gang of sharks! The pirates . . . they've a secret lair in the sunken village . . . You'll need divers to rescue them. But you'll have to be quick, by thunder!

Right, Captain! . . . Piotr, send out a red alert! . . . And Igor, help these men aboard . . .

Meanwhile . . .

O-o-o-h! . . . It's no good! The chains won't break!

Try to pull the pipe away!

In the control room, Rastapopoulos waits . . .

That's it, boss. Our men have shifted all the treasures. It's time we were going. A signal's come through: the police are mounting a tremendous operation.

Good, good . . . I'm coming at once. But first I must change . . .

In the submarine dock the sluices are opened . . .

Ship ready to depart, boss.

The dock fills with water. A lock-gate opens, and the submarine slinks out into the depths of the lake . . .

Once more . . . All together . . . One . . . two . . .

Hooray! . . . Tintin, you're free!

Yes!! . . . But, quick . . . we must get out of here before the whole place blows up!

CRACK

We must hurry! Rastapopoulos wasn't bluffing, that's for sure!

He's locked the door . . . I should have guessed! . . . But we must get out of the cellar. We'll be blown to bits if we don't!

In the submarine . . .

Ha! ha! Just a few minutes more for our clever little friend and . . . WHOOSH! Hundreds of tons of water down on that smart little head!

. . . Nushka, I need a hairpin!

Done it! I've picked the lock! . . . Out we go, quick . . .

CLICK

CLICK

There . . . near the jetty where the submarine brought me in . . . there's an air-lock.

That's our only way out to the surface of the lake.

We'll never make it, Tintin!

There's the air-lock! Put on life-jackets, quickly ... and in we go!

The heavy door sealed behind them, Tintin starts to open the sluices ... the chamber floods rapidly ...

We've made it ... I'm sure ... By a matter of seconds ...

Now, take a deep breath. I'm going to open the gates!

At that moment ...

CLICK

A tremendous explosion rocks every corner of the secret hide-out ...

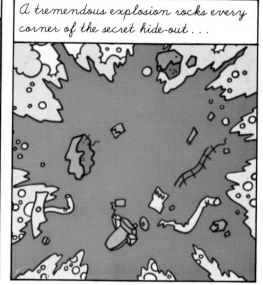

An enormous waterspout pours skywards!

TINTIN!!!

BRROOOOM

HA! HA! Rastapopoulos, you have your revenge! Three jolly prisoners, high in the sky!

OWW!

Dia-vo-lo! ... What ...?!

The blast of the explosion, boss ... I've righted the submarine. Everything's OK now.

Huge waves lash the surface of the lake. The water boils in a sudden storm ... Then, three heads are bobbing in the water ...

Look!! ... Tintin! Niko! Nushka! ... They're alive! ... Quick! The rubber dinghy!

Hang on! I'm coming! ... Captain Haddock to the rescue, blistering barnacles! ...

A second explosion, more violent than the first, shatters the waters of the lake ...

BRROUOUUM

A monstrous wave, a wall of water, looms before the horrified eyes of the swimmers ...

... sucking them under ...

... and with a deafening roar breaks over the helpless police launch ...

For what seems a lifetime, the tiny vessel is buried beneath the churning water... then, miraculously, she shakes herself free.

Billions of blue blistering barnacles!

Ah, we're all washed up!

To be precise, we're a complete washout!

Niko! ... Where is Niko?!

Here! And there's Tintin!

All present and correct, everybody?

Hey! Help us to open the door! It's jammed!

That's the inspector's voice.

Ready! All together now!

CRACK

What about Rastapopoulos and his pirates?

Rastapopoulos! So it was him! Unfortunately, we haven't managed to catch him yet...

...But at least we've picked up some of the sharks. One of our patrols fished out several handsome specimens, and another netted some more when they tried to dump their loot in a cave by the lake.

Inspector, sir! A radio signal!

AAH!

OOH!

TAK - PRAK - PA - TAK

TAK-PARAK-TAK

Hear that, Tintin? The engine's making a very odd noise.

We're not going to break down now, I can tell you!

SPLOTCH

HELP! HELP!

STOP!!

Why, there are the Thompsons . . . water-skiing . . .

WHAT?

Water-skiing?! Billions of bilious blue blistering barnacles!

Tintin goes about and comes to the rescue of the involuntary skiers.

Quick, climb aboard.

Good gracious, no . . . Duty comes first. You carry on . . . We're getting quite used to this sort of thing.

While the detectives swim for the shore, Tintin and the Captain continue their hunt for King Shark.

We don't want to miss that jellyfish when he breaks surface!

Meanwhile . . .

There's the Bordurian shore! . . . We'll keep clear of the frontier posts, and steer straight for the Trident Rocks.

We can't get through that way, boss. Reefs!

Yes, I know all about the reefs . . . and we'll go under them. I worked it all out beforehand, of course! Keep going!

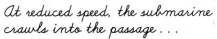

At reduced speed, the submarine crawls into the passage . . .

I'm sure I've forgotten something . . . But what can it be?

THE PERISCOPE!! I've forgotten to lower the periscope!

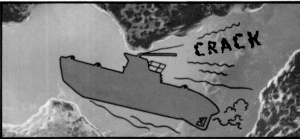

CRACK

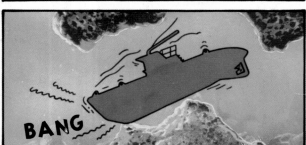

BANG

AAH! The hull is fractured! Quick! Take her up!

Meanwhile . . .

Not a sign . . . I . . . Wait . . . There, beyond the reef! . . . A patch of oil!

. . . It's the submarine! . . . She must be damaged!

They're going to beach her! Quick, Tintin, they mustn't get away!

40

In the submarine, the atmosphere is distinctly tense...

Idiot! It's all your fault! Why didn't you tell me sooner about the periscope, eh?!

But, boss... It was you who...

Shut up! ...You're a fool! And what's more, you're fired!

CRACK

What's happened now?

Hooray! They're stranded! Now we've got them!

So that's how it is, eh? ... OK, you get yourself out of this mess! I'm off!

Stand by to board, by thunder!

Hands up!

AARG!

Oh... oh... b-b-boss... H-h-help... A g-g-g-ghost!

What sort of ghost?!

The g-g-g-ghost of T-t-tin-t-tin!

Tintin! You! . . . You escaped the explosion!!

Yes, King Shark! . . . All right, come on out! Both!

You haven't got me yet!

OH!

Oh yes we have, Rastapopoulos!

Diavolo! . . . Bluebeard! You alive too!

Rastapopoulos and his seamen are soon tied up and taken to the boat.

Heading across the lake, Tintin and the Captain are met by a Syldavian police launch. They and their prisoners are taken aboard. The police convey them safely to the jetty at the Villa Sprog. On shore, a warm reception awaits them! The inspector, Niko, Nushka, the Thompsons, Professor Calculus and of course Gustav and Snowy . . .

Three cheers for Tintin and the Captain!

WOOAH! WOOAH!

The prisoners are taken away to Klow, where the rest of the gang is already in gaol.

Syldavia owes you a great debt, Tintin. Thank you!

WOOAH! GRR

Now we're safe from those gangsters, I can concentrate on my three-dimensional photocopier.

Good! Then you can make me several copies of a very large glass of whisky, Professor!

The village people are coming, sir. They wish to hold a festival in your honour!

News travels fast in these parts, eh?

Thundering typhoons! They're coming from all quarters!

You come and dance a blushtika!

The blushtika?! I . . . er . . . don't know these new-fangled dances!

Come, Tintin. I will teach you. It is very easy!

AAAAAH!!!

♪ ...MY BEAUTY... ♫

Oho! Here comes the Milanese nightingale!

❝...PAST COMPARE!...

GLUB

GLOB

THESE ♫ JEWELS...

How odd... trumpeters sounding the charge?...

♭...BRIGHT...♩

Every man for himself! Blue blistering barnacles! ...The Catastrafiore!

♬...I WEAR!!...♪♪

Dear, dear Captain Bedsock! What a joy to find you safe and well! ... Come, come my pet, and dance with me!

BLUSHTIKA!

BLU-U-SHTIKA!

BLISTERIKA!

To be precise: BLUNDERSTRIKA!

WOOAH!

THE END

44